Lawrence Augustus Gobright

Echoes of Childhood

Old Friends in New Costumes. For the Risen and the Rising Generation

Lawrence Augustus Gobright

Echoes of Childhood
Old Friends in New Costumes. For the Risen and the Rising Generation

ISBN/EAN: 9783337124144

Printed in Europe, USA, Canada, Australia, Japan

Cover: Foto ©Andreas Hilbeck / pixelio.de

More available books at **www.hansebooks.com**

ECHOES OF CHILDHOOD.

OLD FRIENDS IN NEW COSTUMES.

For the Risen and the Rising Generation.

BY

L. A. GOBRIGHT,

AUTHOR OF "RECOLLECTIONS OF MEN AND THINGS AT WASHINGTON," ETC.

" Let us now
With graver air our serious themes pursue,
And yet preserve our moral full in view."— *Francis.*

With Illustrations.

PHILADELPHIA:
CLAXTON, REMSEN & HAFFELFINGER,
624, 626 & 628 MARKET STREET.
1879.

iii

CONTENTS.

INTRODUCTION.

A S children, we have all listened to Mother Goose's Melodies. Their repetition now recalls many happy hours. We then lived in a world of our own. What occurred to us will continue to happen to others. These "jingles," as they have been called, will never cease to delight. The nearer we return to youth, the nearer we reapproach a healthier moral atmosphere than surrounds us in our adult condition. Children, though impulsive, are seldom, if ever, deceitful. They are not included in the exclamation:

> "Oh ! what a tangled web we weave
> When first we practise to deceive."

Peter Parley says: "By a beautiful alchemy of the heart, the clouds of early life appear afterward to be only accessories to the universal springtide of pleasure. In early life all nature is poetry. Childhood and youth are indeed one continuous poem. In most cases this ecstasy of emotion and conception passes away without our special notice. A large portion of it dies out from the memory, but pages are written upon the heart in lines of light and power that cannot be effaced. These become woven into the texture of the soul, and give character to it for time, perchance for eternity. The whole fountain of the mind, like some mineral spring reaching to the interior elements of the earth, is imbued with ingredients which make its current sweet or bitter forever."

Such men as Thackeray and Washington Irving did not regard stories for the nursery as beneath their "distinguished consideration." Thackeray says: "A literary man of the humoristic turn is pretty sure to be of a philosophic nature, to have a great sensibility. to be early moved to pain or pleasure, keenly to appreciate the varieties of temper

INTRODUCTION.

of people round about him, and sympathize in their laughter, love, amusement, tears. Such a man is philosophic, man-loving by nature, as another is irascible, or red-haired, or six feet high. Popular fun is always kind. It is the champion of the humble against the great. In all popular parables, it is little Jack that conquers, and the Giant that topples down. I think that our popular authors are rather hard upon the great folks. Well, well, their lordships have all the money, and can afford to be laughed at."

Washington Irving, in his "Life of Oliver Goldsmith," says: "The world is probably not aware of the ingenuity, humor, good sense, and sly satire contained in many of the English nursery tales. They have evidently been the sportive productions of able writers, who would not trust their names to productions that might be considered beneath their dignity. The ponderous works on which they relied for immortality have perhaps sunk into oblivion, and carried their names down with them, while their unacknowledged offspring, Jack the Giant-killer, Giles Gingerbread, and Tom Thumb, flourish in wide-spreading and never-ceasing popularity."

While the author of the "Echoes of Childhood" admits the improbability of some of the events described in the Nursery Melodies, he nevertheless gives to the narrators due credit for their literary genius, and especially for the affecting story of Jack and Jill, which was several years ago published in a separate volume, and which the author of these pages claimed the right to elaborate, showing the true history of these celebrated personages, and giving the moral to be drawn from their unpretentious lives. So as to the Queen of Hearts, whose lovely character has not heretofore been fully presented to the world. The index to this work will, of course, be consulted, and therefore the author need not specifically call attention to all the characters about whom he speaks with as much sincerity as the facts permit. He has explained many things which are obscure in the original poetry, but has not attempted to improve the text.

INTRODUCTION.

Thus much is due to the intelligent and appreciative reader as an introduction to the historic, traditional, and supposititious things to follow.

The author, with the good-nature which inspires him, permits the public to form its own estimate of the character of this work, while he himself, unaided by modern sons of genius, will seriously discharge his duty to the best of his ability.

To him some of the trifles in the Melodies of Mother Goose seem to be innovations; but as it would be difficult to draw a distinctive line between the genuine and the apocryphal productions, he may be spared from a task involving so much (perhaps fruitless) labor. Therefore he boldly selects from the poetic gems, as texts for his sermons, those which have the greater charm for himself, without attempting to bias the minds of others concerning the simple melodies which have for so many years delighted the young, and which to adults often return as the " Echoes of Childhood " with all their innocent and pleasant memories.

L. A. GOBRIGHT.

WASHINGTON, D. C., October, 1878.

AN INVOCATION!

Now listen to the laughter wild
   Of little girls and boys,
And to the noise of moving feet —
   The chorus of their joys.
If you 're disposed to interfere
   With chilling look or word,
Remember that in childhood you
   Were with like passions stirred.
You can't expect these little folk
   Should be as grave as you,
And their behavior quite as good
   In all they say and do.
A lowance you must make for them,
   And in their sport take part,
And happiness you thus will add
   To many a tender heart.

Story of Jack and Jill

Is usually rendered thus in the modern nursery editions :

> Jack and Jill went up the hill
> To fetch a pail of water,
> When Jack fell down, and broke his crown,
> And Jill came tumbling after.
> Jack up got and home did trot,
> As fast as he could caper;
> His brother Bob plastered his knob
> With vinegar and brown paper.

And in the earlier editions the following verses appeared :

> Little Jane ran up the lane
> To hang the clothes a-drying;
> She called for Nell to ring the bell,
> For Jack and Jill were dying.
> Nimble Dick ran up so quick
> He stumbled over a timber;
> He bent his bow to kill a crow,
> And shot a cat in the window.

PREFACE.

"Because the beginning seemeth abrupt, it needs that you know the occasion of these several adventures, for the method of a poet historical is not such as of an historiographer." — SPENSER.

THE Nursery Melodies which the author has consulted do not give such information concerning the lives of Jack and Jill as he desired to obtain, in order to write their history with the particularity the subject seemed to demand. Mr. Spofford, the chief of the Library of Congress, extended all the facilities in his power to aid the author, who regrets that he is compelled to assert that the literature in that library, though abundant in other respects, is deficient in the matter of Jack and Jill. Therefore, it became necessary to make inquiries elsewhere — among the private, though not extensive libraries of children. But even there the results were not satisfactory. It was found that the several writers of narratives of Jack and Jill do not agree as to the character of the injury to Jack in the fall. They are, however, in harmony on the averment that his head was repaired by the application of " vinegar and brown paper." Taking this for granted, (and the author has, as yet, discovered no one who doubts the truth,) it is unreasonable to suppose that a broken crown could be repaired with such simple appliances! Therefore, the sensible conclusion is that Jack's head was not broken but merely stunned. As to Jack's "capering" to his home, this would seem to be mere poetic license, not warranted by the facts ; or, it may have been intended to cast ridicule on the event which endangered his life !

By a strange mistake, which cannot be explained, the following inappropriate verse was added to the earlier editions of the history :

> " Nimble Dick ran up so quick,
> He stumbled over a timber ;
> He bent his bow to kill a crow,
> And shot a cat in the window."

x

PREFACE.

Evidently this verse belonged to some other story. The fact is so apparent that the author utterly rejects it, without passing an opinion on its poetic merit.

The story of Jack and Jill is as truthfully set forth in these pages as the opportunities for obtaining information warrant; and the author will adhere to this belief until authentic records — not mere logical disquisitions — shall be produced to convince him of mistake!

The name of Jack is from the French *Jacques*, and Latin *Jacobus;* and Jack is the diminutive of John, as understood among ourselves.

Julienne was in vogue among the Norman families. It long prevailed in England as Julyn, and became so common as Gillian that Jill was the regular companion of Jack. We have from this the name of Juliana.

Shakspeare, in his play of the "Midsummer Night's Dream," written about two hundred and seventy-five years ago, alludes to the characters of Jack and Jill; and Ray, in his "Proverbs," speaks of them in a pleasant way; the latter asserting, as a truth, that "a good Jack makes a good Jill;" which fact is illustrated in these pages.

Ben Jonson, in his "Gypsies," says:

> "I can, for I will,
> Here at Burley o' the hill,
> Give you all your fill,
> Each Jack with his Jill."

In a note to "Specimens of Lyric Poems," composed in England during the reign of Edward the First, six hundred years ago, it is said there was an old play, now lost, called "Jack and Jill."

Researches show that King James I. of Scotland, who died in 1437, wrote the poem of "Christ's Kirk on the Green," from which it appears that *Gillie* scorned and made mouths at *Jok;* which treatment, to say the least, was unkind, and that Jok "would have loved Gillie" but "she would not let him." This statement cannot refer to our Jack and Jill, unless, by an extension of the imagination, it can be supposed that Gillie

PREFACE.

was finally " brought to terms " by Jok, as is sometimes the case in love adventures. It is certain, however, that the royal bard selected these two euphonic names to adorn his poetry, and has linked them with imperishable fame!

The author affectionately requests the readers of this poem to believe that he has undertaken to reconcile probabilities with facts, while discarding the absurdities of compilers, his object being to restore the history to its original seriousness !

> " 'Tis not indeed my talent to engage
> In lofty trifles, or to swell my page
> With wind and noise."

For centuries the simple story of Jack and Jill has delighted millions upon millions of children, who, in after years, did not forget the narrative. It has always been pleasant to recall the story, and so it will continue to be in coming time, as long as there is a child in Christendom with the ability to understand the oral relation of the story, or to read it without adult assistance.

The author submits his poem, not to public criticism, but to the judgment of all who appreciate contributions to literature, and especially as his production will, he is sure, fill a vacancy in the libraries of the world, provided the history of Jack and Jill be not rejected in consequence of the ridicule heretofore thoughtlessly cast upon their names!

The narrative should have a place appropriate to the merits of the humble characters never to be separated from English and American memories. The author is certain that the poem will adorn the Library of Congress, as the law requires two specimens of all copyrighted works to be placed within its sacred keeping!

L. A. GOBRIGHT.

JACK AND JILL.

———◦∶◦∶◦◦———

CHAPTER I.

I N literature we 've Jack and Jill,
 Preserved in nursery rhyme,
Of interest now to young and old,
 As in the ancient time.

It is not told where they were born,
 Or who their parents were,
But certain 't is they parents had,
 Who nurtured them with care,

And fitted them as best they could
 To lead a happy life,
That Jack a husband good should be,
 And Jill a model wife.

13

Now, in the walk of humble life,
    And in their married state,
The great and small alike may find
    Much good to imitate.

"John Anderson, my Jo John,"
    A song which you've heard often,
Which will henceforth, as in the past,
    The soul's best feelings soften,

Tells how John climbed the hill of life,
    By blessings rich attended,
And to the vale, without a fall,
    With his good wife descended.

Alas! not so with reference
    To rustic Jack and Jill,
Who went up slower than they came
    Adown the slippery hill!

From this Burns, maybe, made his song,
    Much everywhere admired,
With such improvements as his Muse
    And kindly heart inspired.

The city has its gayety,
  Where wealth and thrift abound,
And vice and virtue, strongly marked,
  In neighborhood are found.

But many love the country more,
  With its untainted air,
The woodland, and the field, and lawn
  And better morals there.

And in this rural life are hearts
  Which do not vices know;
But virtues which mankind adorn,
  And happiness bestow.

More rich are they with grateful hearts,
  From which contentment springs,
Than those whose e'er increasing wealth
  No true enjoyment brings.

Jack led a strictly moral life,
  Which was a theme of praise,
And everybody wished that he
  Could follow in Jack's ways.

He did not ardent spirits drink
  For artificial cheer,
But was contented with supplies
  Of Jill's refreshing beer.

He ne'er neglected Mrs. Jill,
  Nor close attention paid
To any neighbor's pretty wife,
  Or any comely maid.

No tenpin alley, sample room,
  Or vulgar concert hall,
Could him from his domestic state
  And occupation call.

He owned a little tract of ground,
  To which he gave his toil,
And was rewarded with the fruits
  That issued from the soil.

His cot was plain, but neatly kept
  By Jill, with humble pride,
Who freely whitewash used within
  And on the boards outside.

She planted flower-seeds in the yard,
  Near to the cottage-gate,
And paid attention to the soil
  That they might germinate.

The generous earth its beauties gave,
  Rare, odorous, profuse,
With all the primal colors
  And their secondary hues.

Her cabbages and onions were
  The best her neighbors knew,
With other culinary plants
  Which in her garden grew.

She fed her fowl, she milked her cow,
  And everywhere 'twas said
No woman in the country round
  Such bread and butter made.

In all she did, indoors or out,
  She showed good taste and skill,
Which Jack her husband seconded
  With ready act and will.

CHAPTER II.

Domestic Comfort — Rural Luxury — Proof of Affection — Going for
the Water — The Drink — The Circumstances attending the
Fall — Misfortunes from a Cooling Draught, etc.

IN time of summer Jack and Jill,
   Their dinner being o'er,
Sat down to talk and rest themselves
   Before their cottage-door.

The shower that brightened tree and grass
   Had cooled the heated air,
And light winds through the clover-bloom
   Conveyed its fragrance there.

Said Jill "I thirst, I want a drink
   Drawn from our favorite spring,
When Jack replied " I'll water get,
   If you a vessel bring."

Responsive to Jack's readiness
   His loving Jill supplied
The pail, which had been lately scoured,
   And placed it at his side.

As little Mary had a lamb,
  Whose fleece was white, like snow,
And wheresoever Mary went
  The lamb was sure to go;

Jill with devotion quite as strong
  Attended on her Jack,
Who always found her at his side
  Or closely at his back.

Said she " I'll go along with you,
  To cheer you on the way,
Because I care not at this place
  Without my Jack to stay."

Then up they went the hillside steep
  The water to obtain,
And with this purpose at the spring
  No longer to remain.

They took a deep and cooling drink,
  And filled the wooden pail,
But on returning to their cot
  Departed from the trail.

Their eyes were turned toward Nature's charms,
  Extending all around,
With dotting flowers upon her robes
  And by the greenwood bound.

Birds resting in their leafy homes
  From weariness of flight,
Upon the beauteous scene looked forth
  And warbled with delight.

The ground being wet with recent rain
  And slippery to the tread,
Jack fell adown the steep hillside
  And struck upon his head!

Jill screamed like any other wife
  Who for her husband feels,
But in her haste to reach her Jack
  She tumbled at his heels.

Alas! this shows that in an hour
  When mortals little think
Misfortune will upon them come
  E'en from a cooling drink!

CHAPTER III.

What Jill did after the Accident — Timely Arrival of Assistance —
The Alarm — Tolling of the Bell — Wonderful Effects of Vinegar
and Brown Paper — The Recovery — The Lesson.

WHEN Jill arose and cried for help,
    Which very soon was found,
The neighbors handled Jack with care
    And raised him from the ground;

Then bore him to his cottage home
    And placed him in his bed,
While words gave way to silent grief
    And tears were freely shed.

The news soon spread, both far and near;
    The villagers, alarmed,
Rushed wildly to the scene to learn
    If Jack was sorely harmed!

'Twas then that little Jane, who 'd just
    Put out her clothes to dry,
Tore her blonde hair and wrung her hands
    As she began to cry.

She thought Jack dead, and in her grief
   Implored her sister Nell
To hasten to the village church
   And forthwith toll the bell.

Ah! 'twas a time of deepest woe
   To poor Jack's every friend,
Who thought that he had by the fall
   Come to a fatal end!

Jack had a brother very kind,
   Bob was his common name;
Soon as he heard the tolling bell
   With breathless haste he came.

And bending o'er his brother Jack,
   Feeling his head with care,
He was rejoiced to find no bump
   Nor any fracture there!

Jack gave a sign which showed that he
   Was not among the dead,
And while he groaned in deep distress
   He pointed to his head.

25

It thus appeared Jack was but stunned —
  E'en this was much deplored —
And that by simple remedies
  He soon might be restored.

Brown paper, steeped in vinegar,
  With confidence was tried,
And was by Bob with tender hand
  To Jack's hurt head applied.

This had a wonderful effect,
  And brought to Jack relief;
There now was no excuse for tears
  Or utterance of grief!

The neighbors all rejoiced that Jack
  Was without any pain,
Or even scratch, and hoped that he
  Would ne'er fall down again!

Jack, now restored to cheerful health,
  Industrious was found,
Attending to his faithful Jill
  And to his farming ground.

He lived for many years in peace
  And happiness with Jill;

Their children meantime played upon
  But ne'er fell down the hill!

Since these events proud governments
  Of glory have been shorn,
And others disappeared in gloom,
  With few the loss to mourn;

While nations weak have grown in strength,
  And e'en our own had birth,
The freest and the happiest
  Existing on the earth.

Though countless names illuminate
  The history of man,
For warlike acts and civic deeds
  E'er since the world began,

No characters are better known
  Than humble Jack and Jill,
With incidents concerning them
  That happened on the hill.

From which a lesson may be learned,
  Of interest to all:
Let them who think they firmly stand
  Take warning lest they fall!

The Reign of Hearts.

The original text reads as follows in the Melodies.

"The Queen of Hearts
She made some tarts
All on a summer's day;
The Knave of Hearts
He stole the tarts,
And with them ran away.

"The King of Hearts
Called for those tarts,
And beat the Knave full sore;
The Knave of Hearts
Brought back the tarts,
And vowed he'd steal no more."

THE REIGN OF HEARTS.

—oo⟩⦿⟨oo—

CHAPTER I.

THE Queen a good example set,
 And, scorning all things vain,
She sought to render happier
 Her husband's peaceful reign.

"Industrious be," her motto was
 To classes rich and poor,
"If you would always plenty have
 In basket and in store."

The Queen, to show proficiency
 In the domestic arts,
Descended to the kitchen's gloom
 To manufacture tarts.

It mattered not, though summer time,
  And Sirius fiercely raged,
With nimble white and jewelled hands
  She in the work engaged.

And when the labor, self-imposed,
  Successfully was o'er,
She placed the tarts, that they might cool,
  Outside the kitchen door.

Her right to rule the kitchen realm
  By industry was earned;
But, ah! the tarts could not be found
  When she for them returned.

The Knave of Hearts, secreted near,
  A thief by night and day,
Had pounced upon the tempting tarts
  And with them ran away!

The Queen, discovering she 'd been robbed,
  The fact told to the King,
Who sent a guard to catch the Knave,
  And him to judgment bring.

With his left hand the irate King
  Seized by the throat the Knave,
And with a cudgel in his right
  Severe instruction gave.

"Go now and bring to me the tarts
  Made by my model wife;
A failure to obey my word
  Involves your worthless life!"

The Knave retired, and soon returned,
  Obeying the command,
And forthwith placed the savory tarts
  Within the royal hand.

The Sovereign ate, and thanked the Queen
  For the good tarts she made;
The Knave meantime asunder stood,
  Confounded and afraid!

Then falling at the royal feet
  To amnesty implore,
The Knave declared with tearful eyes
  He'd depredate no more.

CHAPTER II.

The Lesson of Charity Taught by the Queen — The Plea for Pardon — The Queen Triumphant — The King's Proclamation — The Reign of Hearts.

WE know 'mong woman's brightest gems
  Are acts of tenderness
T'ward those who suffer and are known
  As objects of distress;

Therefore the Queen, in gentle tones,
  Spoke to her generous lord,
Convinced the gracious boon she asked
  He gladly would accord.

"My liege," she said, "forgive the crime,
  And pardon now declare,
For in the joy such deeds bestow
  My heart will ever share.

"All human beings may at times
  The moral precepts break;
But while we should condemn the wrong,
  We need not vengeance take."

The King replied, " I 've heard your prayer,
   My faithful Queen of Hearts,
But I 'm reluctant to forgive
   The crime of stealing tarts.

" 'T is for your sake alone I yield,
   I can't resist the prayer
So full of generous sentiment,
   And pardon now declare ! "

At his command up rose the Knave
   Who stole the tempting tarts,
And in excess of gratitude
   Extolled the reign of Hearts!

The Queen of Hearts, though victor now,
   Did not attempt to speak,
Save in the tears of thankfulness
   That glistened on her cheek;

And clinging to the jewelled neck
   Of him who wrong forgave,
She kissed the lips that had declared
   Full pardon to the Knave!

The King returned the warm caress
  And kisses of his wife,
Who, by example, taught him how
  To lead a happier life.

The charity that joyousness
  In thought and deed imparts,
Should have its dwelling everywhere,
  Including royal hearts!

MR. AND MRS. SPRATT.

"Jack Spratt could eat no fat,
    His wife could eat no lean;
      So, nothing loth,
      Between them both
    They licked the platter clean."

A valuable lesson to husbands and wives, showing that compromise preserves the peace.

MAY peace prevail forevermore
    In the domestic state,
With no discordant elements
    Nor words to irritate.

'Tis known Concord and Harmony
    To tender hearts are bound,
And are alike in palaces
    And humble dwellings found.

The world is better than do say
    Those who of it complain,
But, notwithstanding, cherish hopes
    To longer here remain!

Within ourselves the secret lies
  Of happiness or woe,
And with the culture of the heart
  The fruits of love will grow.

Neglected, Vice will silently,
  And by degrees, obtain
The mastery, and there, perhaps,
  Forever will remain.

Sometimes a man will suffer pain
  In consequence of deeds
Which, step by step, in his career
  To further trouble leads.

It may be that he can't escape
  The public's searching gaze,
Who 're always ready to condemn
  And stigmatize his ways.

Amid the perils that surround,
  Whate'er their nature be,
Let every one, to guard his fame,
  Act as his own trustee.

Let character be always built
  Upon a moral base,
Which storms detractive cannot move
  Or injure with disgrace!

Slight causes, like the little cloud,
  Presage the storm to come,
When darkness in the place of light
  Rests densely over home.

But, unlike nature, with her storms,
  Which purify the air,
Domestic ones the household taint
  And leave no blessing there!

Self-will, the sovereign of the mind,
  Is oft the cause of strife,
Whether the husband be to blame,
  Or resting with the wife.

No woman is content the man
  Shall of his food complain,
Or unbecomingly intrude
  Upon the cook's domain;

And neither should insist the meal,
  Without a scrap of waste,
Be measured to the appetite,
  Exactly to the taste.

Accommodation works its good,
  And will disputes defeat;
This fact is found in nursery lore
  About a piece of meat.

A rustic, Jacky Spratt, was joined
  To a fair country maid,
But during courtship not a word
  About their fare was said.

Love was the power within their hearts
  Which them together drew,
And made them one as man and wife —
  As such they happier grew.

One day was cooked a piece of meat,
  As good as e'er was seen —
A half was of the purest fat,
  The other half was lean.

'T is said that Jack rejected fat,
    Could not the substance eat;
And that his wife discarded lean
    From the same piece of meat!

The narrative 's not clear to those
    Who ever truth pursue,
But simple reason must supply
    The facts obscured from view.

It is: the lean passed to the mouth
    Of Mr. Jacky Spratt,
And that his wife the portion ate
    Distinctly marked as fat.

Because we cannot think they 'd waste
    The meat which health required,
When both were hungry, and could eat
    What each the most desired.

The tastes diverse thus gratified
    In eating fat and lean,
They closed the meal harmoniously
    And "licked the platter clean!"

It would not well become us now
    To criticize their ways,
Nor venture comments, or express
    Our censure or our praise.

We take the bare recited truth,
    The homely stated act,
And nothing add or take away
    From the recorded fact.

Of this there's nothing to be said
    That's classic or refined,
But we must recollect that they
    Were of uncultured mind!

Besides, what they did at their board
    Concerned themselves, not those
Whose tongues in scandal fierce indulge
    And seldom know repose.

The lesson's this: when tastes diverse
    With comforts interfere,
Think of Jack Spratt and of his wife,
    And of their dinner cheer.

LITTLE MISS MUFFIT AND THE SPIDER.

"Little Miss Muffit
    Sat on a tuffit,
Eating curds and whey;
    There came out a spider
    And sat down beside her,
And frightened Miss Muffit away!"

SOMETIMES, when we contented are,
    Partaking of our food,
Unlooked for creatures may appear
    And on the feast intrude.

No matter if the fare be plain,
    Such are bread and cheese,
And curds and whey, and mush and milk,
    The appetite to please,

We love to eat with cheerful mind,
   And with no sense of fear
That any form repulsively
   Will at the board appear.

An ancient Hebrew monarch said
   A dinner e'en of herbs,
If charity but season it,
   And nothing wrong disturbs,

Is better than a stalléd ox
   Served as a generous meal,
If those who eat possess not love,
   But only hatred feel.

No wonder that Miss Muffit, while
   Intent upon her fare,
Was frightened by a spider vile
   That sat beside her there!

The lady's dread to feel its bite
   Opposed her longer stay,
And rather than its company keep
   She from it ran away!

While she could have the spider killed,
  Thus ending its career,
Perhaps she did not think of this,
  So potent was her fear.

But if she had the insect crushed
  Without the least delay,
She might have, without further fear,
  Consumed her curds and whey.

Though we should never cruel be,
  And kill for trifling cause,
The subtle prisoner should not
  Escape the penal laws.

Are not mosquitoes sometimes killed
  In sultry summer night,
While in the act of drawing blood,
  In which they take delight?

Are not snakes slain that move in grass
  And dart the hissing tongue,
In anxious gladness for the prey
  To be with poison stung?

But, if they 'd keep away, no club,
    Or other deadly thing,
Would interrupt them in their ways
    Or swift destruction bring!

There 're spiders in this lower world
    That ever watch for prey,
Both in the covert of the night
    And in the open day.

No matter what the form may be
    Of all pestiferous things,
Whether they upon two legs walk,
    Or crawl, or move with wings,

The safer and the better way
    Is so to act our part
That they shall not our bodies harm,
    Or vitiate the heart!

THE OLD WOMAN UNDER THE HILL.

A LESSON OF HUMILITY.

"There was an old woman lived under a hill,
And if she's not gone she lives there still."

HER home was not a mansion large,
  With windows broad and high,
And ample grounds and ornaments
  Which riches could supply.

But how she lived, or kind of house,
  The poet does not state:
This seemed a trifle in his mind
  That he does not relate.

'Tis not narrated she'd such kin,
  And therefore trouble knew,
Like one who many children had
  And lived within a shoe.

47

The poet briefly speaks of her
    As though she lived alone,
With no romance upon herself
    Or habitation thrown.

The fact that she her domicile
    Under the hillside made,
Not in the sun's exposing blaze,
    But in the softened shade,

Shows that she lived an humble life,
    Which envy could not reach,
And that her ways, unheralded,
    Should e'er contentment teach.

Perhaps a widow's lot was hers,
    By loneliness oppressed,
But with the wealth in faith and hope
    By pious hearts possessed.

The flowers that grow in summer's shade
    Do not such hardness bear
As those which to the north winds bow
    And in the sunbeams share.

But tender flowers their beauty have
  In modesty's array,
Though they do not strong odors yield
  Nor gorgeous tints display.

So, worthy deeds of human kind
  Performed, though in the shade,
Should not be valued less than those
  With brighter light displayed.

The poet briefly tells to us,
  In unpretending rhyme,
Where the old nameless lady lived,
  But does not state the time.

The fact implies that all who live
  Must quite as surely die,
And the remains of those we love
  Beneath the hillock lie.

We can't the poet's story doubt
  That underneath the hill
The woman old, "if she's not gone,"
  Has there her dwelling still!

LITTLE POLLY FLINDERS.

"Little Polly Flinders
Sat among the cinders,
Warming her pretty little toes;
Her mother came and caught her,
And whipped her little daughter
For spoiling her nice new clothes!"

MISS Polly Flinders, being cold,
The warming cinders sought,
Not thinking that her conduct was
With castigation fraught.

She sat the cinders bright among,
Regardless of her clothes,
Because her object was to warm
Her pretty little toes!

The mother had with care and taste
  Her only daughter dressed;
The clothes were new she gave to her,
  From stinted means the best.

Poor Polly, like a thoughtless child,
  Did not perceive, though vain,
The sacrifice the mother made
  The garments to obtain.

Like children of a larger growth,
  She loved to take her ease;
Nor dreamed warmth from the cinders' glare
  The mother would displease.

But she was waked to consciousness
  By her dame's startling voice,
Which did not to her comfort bring
  Nor make her heart. rejoice!

The clothing formed in fashion's mould
  Was by the cinders soiled
And partly burned, as were her shoes,
  And thus completely spoiled!

As heedlessness oft trouble brings
   From which there's no relief,
Poor little Polly felt with force
   The measure of her grief.

This was not all; the angry dame
   To her full height arose,
And Polly whipped because she spoiled
   Her nicely fitting clothes.

Now, Conscience may apart from this
   All evil-doers chide,
And this is more severe than blows
   With stick or hardened hide!

THE LANCASHIRE BOY.

"Little boy, little boy,
    Where wast thou born?
Far off in Lancashire,
    Under a thorn,
Where they sup sour milk in a ram's horn."

IT matters little where a child
    First sees the solar light,
For this alone no difference makes,
    If other things are right.

We know the training of a child
    Controls his future days,
Whether it be in ignorance
    Or wisdom's pleasant ways.

All men look back, but not with shame,
  To certain parts of earth,
Because an interest always clings
  To places of their birth.

The boy of whom the poet speaks
  In Lancashire was born:
Not in a palace or an inn,
  But underneath a thorn.

No silver spoon within his mouth
  Accompanied his advent,
For this is not the implement
  With humble offspring sent.

No cup or bowl of precious ware
  Was seen where he was born,
But for imbibing sour milk
  A ram supplied a horn.

Men are not worse for sour milk,
  Which none perhaps suppose,
No more than they are injured by
  The color of their clothes.

55

While some men may select with care
　The food on which they live,
'T is folly if the food they eat
　Sound bodies does not give.

Every one should eat and drink
　What best with him agrees,
Not asking whether certain fare
　Would *all* his neighbors please.

If others turn from sour milk,
　Let them drink milk that's sweet;
And if they don't love pork or lamb,
　Take other kinds of meat.

All to their taste in everything,
　Minding their own affairs,
And this would save them from distress
　And many trifling cares.

DOMESTIC CONTENTION ABOUT MONEY.

"My little old woman and I fell out;
I'll tell you what 't was all about:
I had money and she had none,
And that's the way the noise begun."

A MAN'S good-natured while his wife
  Yields her will to his own;
Ill words and loud complaints not then
  Are to the household known.

But he cannot expect her e'er
  To bow a willing head,
And hold her tongue, nor contradict
  What may by him be said!

Now if he venture very far,
    And think he owns his wife,
She, in assertion of her rights,
    May cause a mournful life.

A couple close in social bonds,
    An aged man and wife,
Forgetful of their marriage vows,
    Engaged in noisy strife.

'T is said that money she possessed,
    And he not e'en a cent,
Because he all his currency
    In dissipation spent.

He sought to draw upon his wife,
    By her to be supplied
With cash, but this she valiantly
    And earnestly denied.

If 't was her own, she had the right
    To him refuse the pelf;
And if he wanted some, he should
    Have earned it for himself!

THE THREE WISE MEN!

—◦◦✕◦◦—

"Three wise men of Gotham
Went to sea in a bowl.
If the bowl had been stronger,
My story would have been longer."

The narrative shows that the example of wise men is
not always worthy of imitation.

———

THREE men of Gotham, ere had clouds
From steamer swept the main,
Resorted to a novel plan
Their object to attain.

Perhaps they searched for knowledge rare
Found in aquatic lore,
And wished to gaze on ocean's face
Unbounded by the shore!

59

They were not foolish men, because
 We're told that they were wise,
And hence their travelling means should be
 No matter of surprise.

These three wise men could never have,
 With all their learning, heard
About the pot launched on the stream,
 And what to it occurred.

'T was made of iron, and had been used
 The dinner fare to cook;
Though bright within, its outside had
 A thickly-blackened look.

The owner, seeking t' other shore,
 Entered the rotund shell,
Which foundered with its human freight,
 And to the bottom fell!

The question need not be discussed,
 Though 't is a serious theme,
Whether a pot to reach the sea
 Was quite as good a scheme

As was the bowl the wise men used
  Without a canvas wing,
Depending on the favoring waves
  To waft their fragile thing!

It is, however, a settled fact,
  That he who tries the feat
Of travelling in a dinner-pot
  Will no more dinners eat!

Attempts like this to reach the sea
  Can't with success be crowned;
And such a man, if he can't swim,
  Must certainly be drowned!

Beyond all cavil and dispute,
  Liquids will e'er control
Not only that known to the sea,
  But in the pot or bowl.

And when men much indulge in drink,
  They venture on a wave
Which with their bowl will float them on
  To early fill a grave.

Experimenters oft receive
  Affliction for their pay,
And sometimes in schemes dangerous
  Their life is ta'en away.

All men would better fare if they
  Would recollect one thing:
The breach of Nature's laws will e'er
  Chastisement surely bring.

The ignorant should not condemn
  The actions of wise men,
For 't is supposed that men who 're wise
  All useful knowledge ken.

'T would have been folly in a tar
  To his experience give,
Because these wise men thought a bowl
  Could on the ocean live!

That mountain waves could only move
  The shell which they employed,
And that by floods and winds combined
  It could not be destroyed!

While these wise men by going out
   A lasting record earned,
The story does not say that they
   Home in the bowl returned.

They learned the truth when 't was too late,
   That they could not control
The winds, nor save from surging sea
   Themselves within the bowl!

So thus went down beneath the waves
   Wise men of Gotham three;
And none have since employed a bowl
   In which to cross the sea.

MUSIC FOR THE MILLION.

"The man that hath no music in himself,
 Nor is not moved with concord of sweet sounds,
 Is fit for treasons, stratagems, and spoils;
 The motions of his spirit are dull as night,
 And his affections dark as Erebus.
 Let no such man be trusted."—*Shakspeare.*

"Tom, Tom, the piper's son,
  Stole a pig, and away he run;
    The pig was eat
    And Tom was beat,
  And Tom ran crying down the street."

SHAKSPEARE, whose works will ever be
  A treasure to mankind,
Because they wise instruction give
  And elevate the mind,

Relates the mournful state of those,
  With callousness of soul,
Who ne'er are moved by melody
  Or feel its sweet control.

A piper lived — we don't know where —
  But he his music played,
And by this unpretentious means
  An humble living made.

The sounds were simple, yet they could
  Admiring tongues command,
So good were the selected airs
  And skilled the player's hand.

The village boasted that it had
  An instrumental voice;
A pipe, though speaking to the ear,
  Could make the heart rejoice.

There was among the listeners
  One being only found,
Who had no taste for harmony
  Or pipe's melodious sound.

Alas! but the most serious thing
  That could be said or done,
Was this exception to the rule
  Was in the piper's son!

Tom had no music in his soul —
  'T was not congenial soil —
Therefore he was prepared for theft,
  Or other kind of spoil!

His tastes were of the lowest kinds,
  His thoughts with plunder big,
To the extent he stooped to mire
  And stole a neighbor's pig!

Then sold it to a victualler,
  A dealer in such meat,
Who bought it in a business way,
  Unconscious of the cheat.

But soon the owner of the pig
  The thief a captive made,
And, scornful of the law's delay,
  Hard blows upon him laid.

The thief, exposed to public gaze,
　And his disgrace complete,
Not knowing where to hide his shame,
　Ran crying down the street.

We do not say that all who have
　No love for music's might,
Would steal a pig or other thing,
　Or moral duties slight;

But that the love of melody
　Will pleasure e'er impart,
And serve to turn the mind from crime
　And better make the heart.

Though some men, in dyspeptic mood,
　Are rude toward the poor
Itinerant who daily brings
　His music to the door,

The children flock to hear the tunes
　The organist repeats,
If, 'specially, a monkey dance,
　With other comic feats.

Amid the pleasure, free to all,
　　It is not known the young
Believe with Darwin that mankind
　　From apes or monkeys sprung!

While gentlemen and ladies fill
　　At prices high the chairs
In theatres and music halls,
　　To list to foreign airs,

Let music for the million sound
　　In avenues and streets,
The joy of all the juveniles,
　　With no exclusive seats;

Where there is standing room for all,
　　Without regard to age,
With no corrupting tendencies
　　Reflected from the stage!

THE BOY AND THE OWL.

"A little boy went into a barn,
  And lay down on some hay;
An owl came out and flew about,
  And the little boy ran away."

A LITTLE boy, fatigued with play,
    A quiet rest desired,
And therefore he to gain that end
  To a barn-house retired.

He did not think of going home,
  Perhaps 't was far away;
Besides, when weary, beds of down
  Are not more choice than hay.

Contented with the quiet barn,
  With no disturbing things,
He in that barn was happier
  Than Presidents or Kings!

71

The drooping body must have rest
　Where 't is the soonest found,
Whether within a sheltered place
　Or on the grass-clad ground.

The boy upon his bed of hay
　Surrounded with perfume,
Inhaled the odor of the field
　Fresh with the clover bloom.

But oftentimes when we believe
　Ourselves the most secure
From troubles and perplexing cares,
　Unpleasant acts inure.

The boy was not disturbed by dog,
　Or any barn-yard fowl,
But by a bird of homely mien —
　A rude, intruding owl!

Which thought (if such birds think at all)
　'T was trespass in the boy
To come into the barn and there
　A quiet rest enjoy.

It did not to the owl occur
    Its verdict was unfair,
Because the bird had not itself
    A rightful presence there.

'Tis certain that it could not urge
    Good looks as its defence,
Or that, in contrast with the boy,
    It had more common sense.

Presuming on its night-time fame,
    It wildly flew about
To make the boy afraid to stay,
    And from the barn run out!

'Tis said that wisdom in the owl
    Is as an emblem found,
Though reasons satisfactory
    For this claim don't abound.

We know, howe'er, pretentiousness
    Has always too much sway,
And, like the owl, offensively
    Flaps modest worth away!

THE

EQUESTRIENNE OF BANBURY CROSS.

"Ride a cock horse to Banbury Cross,
  To see an old lady on a white horse;
  Rings on her fingers and bells on her toes,
  She shall have music wherever she goes."

OCCURRENCES upon the street,
  Though in their features trite,
Will often draw a wondering crowd
  To gratify the sight.

E'en should a person upward look,
  But at no certain thing,
This if continued for a while
  Will other gazers bring.

74

The curious are e'er alert
  Some novelty to find,
Whether to gratify the eye
  Or stimulate the mind.

The feet are swift to carry some
  Upon their chosen course,
Who do not for a moment think
  Of travelling with a horse;

While others, better circumstanced,
  And having money means,
Resort to nag or vehicle
  To reach exciting scenes.

The taste for such divertisements
  Attached to those who hied
To Banbury, a dame to see
  Upon a white horse ride!

Without a question she was vain,
  And eager to display
Her golden finger-rings with gems
  That sparkled to the day.

And silver bells of various notes
  To all her toes she bound,
So that where'er in pride she moved
  Was heard a tinkling sound.

The crowd, delighted, cheered the dame
  While mounting on her steed,
And then beheld her fearlessly
  Far in the distance speed.

The concourse broke, and many wights
  Ran o'er the dusty course,
Believing that they could o'ertake
  The lady on the horse!

Soon she returned to Banbury Cross,
  Apparently as gay
As when first 'mid the loud acclaim
  She started on her way.

And capering on her foaming steed,
  She to the people bowed,
And with triumphant smiles received
  The plaudits of the crowd.

'T is novelty that e'er attracts
  And close attention brings,
While useful knowledge is ignored
  For merely trifling things.

Men now, as in the ancient days,
  The many, not the few,
Are asking friends with eagerness
  To show them something new!

THE DYSPEPSIA CURE.

"There was an old man of Tobago,
 Who lived on rice, gruel, and sago,
   Till much to his bliss,
   IIis physician said this:
'To a leg, sir, of mutton you may go.'"

VARIETY'S the spice of life,"
   By all so understood,
And to the body and the mind
   Will ever render good.

The eagle in a golden cage
   Would be considered poor,
If he could not the barriers break
   And in the sunlight soar.

His pleasures are in actions free,
   With strong and graceful wing,
And in the unrestricted food
   His depredations bring.

No one should think because a man
   Must walk, and cannot fly,
Therefore a sumptuary law
   Should certain fare deny.

Strange fact, that while historians
   Important deeds relate,
They do not think it worth their while
   The actors' names to state.

But we're told of one who lived
   Long time, without a smile,
At Tobago, euphonic name,
   A small West India isle,

And that his food was cheap and plain —
   Gruel, sago, and rice —
Which would not be by epicures
   Considered very nice.

Dyspepsia's torments made him sad
   And cross to all around,
But as a curative the leech
   Him to a diet bound.

He did not overphysic him
  With liquid or with pill,
And to the doctor's charges add
  A drug-compounding bill;

But slowly helped him on his way
  Till his disease was o'er,
Then placed him with a knife and fork
  A mutton leg before!

No groans and sobs, and loud complaints,
  And vile and profane word,
Which in the past escaped from him,
  Were ever after heard.

The mutton feast restored his smiles
  And laughter; these things tell
Better than other signs
  When men are really well.

The simple lesson seems to be
  Designed alone for those
Who by imprudence bring upon
  Themselves dyspeptic woes.

Here's a prescription for their ills,
  Bestowed without a fee,
Which, if observed, from such disease
  Will set the patient free;

Combined with effort to divert
  His mind from sense of pain,
With constant hope that cheerful health
  Will soon return again.

One need not try the medicines
  Which empirics prepare
For cure of all the ills to which
  The human flesh is heir.

Wild, hearty laughter always proves
  A source of mental wealth,
And light amusements ever serve
  To re-establish health.

Long faces ill become mankind
  In these enlightened days,
But rather smiles and kindly words
  And good and pleasant ways.

COURTSHIP—LOVE'S ARGUMENT.

"Bonny lass, bonny lass,
    Wilt thou be mine?
You shall neither wash dishes
    Nor serve the wine,
But sit on a cushion
    And sew up a seam,
And you shall have strawberries,
    Sugar and cream."

THE gallant, with a honeyed tongue,
    One of a numerous class,
Resorts to tender expletives,
    Such as "My bonny lass!"

And finding that the lady thinks
    They are of love the sign,
He boldly presses on his suit,
    And asks, "Wilt thou be mine?"

82

Not waiting for a sweet response
    Expressive of her wishes,
He tells her she the wine sha'n't serve,
    Nor wash the dinner-dishes;

But sit upon a cushioned chair,
    The needle nimbly ply,
As if this were the only work
    On which she should rely.

If sewing instruments had been
    The fashion in that day,
He would have promised that she might
    In buying have her way,

And be at liberty to choose
    That which she thought the best,
With shuttle, or the underfeed,
    Or needle-hook the test;

With the facilities to quilt,
    Hem, ruffle, frill and braid,
By means of the contrivances
    So delicately made.

Further, to win the prize he sought,
　　And keep her as his own,
He tells her of the only food
　　That should to them be known.

Not fare that's coarse, that could disturb
　　The lady's pleasant dream,
But strawberries with sugar sprent
　　And intermixed with cream!

With ease such promises are made
　　The wedding-time before;
And, ah! that is the last of them —
　　They're never mentioned more.

The bridal o'er, the rosy tints
　　O'er youthful prospects thrown
Depart, like bubbles by a breath
　　From pipes with soapsuds blown!

THE WISE-FOOLISH MAN!

"There was a man in our town,
And he was wondrous wise;
He jumped into a bramble-bush
And scratched out both his eyes."

THIS illustrates a man, though wise,
  May do a foolish thing,
Which will disturb his equipoise
And sorrow to him bring.

In cases ninety-nine he will
  Discharge all duties right,
But in the hundredth either fail
Or their performance slight.

"But when he saw his eyes were out,
  He ran with might and main
And jumped into another bush
And scratched them in again."

When he reflects upon his course,
　And what he thereby lost,
He seriously deliberates
　And strictly counts the cost.

Then he resolves to mend his ways
　And rid his heart of pain;
Returning to his former ways
　He sees himself again.

Alas! too many gentlemen
　Are from good habits torn,
And ne'er return to them again
　Till by reflection borne.

LITTLE JACK HORNER.

"Little Jack Horner
Sat in a corner,
Eating his Christmas pie;
He put in his thumb
And pulled out a plum,
And said, "What a good boy am I?"

WE'VE heard of Jacky Horner
And of his Christmas pie,
The lad that gladly feasted on
The holiday supply,

And even where the youngster sat
At that particular time;
But this fact is related merely
To complete the rhyme.

Now the exploit that he performed
  Was nothing very smart;
No more than if he had then ta'en
  A cranberry from a tart!

He claimed his goodness from a plum
  That he drew from the mess;
Beyond this act no merit did
  He venture to express!

This is the way that many have,
  Too numerous to name,
Who for their trite performances
  Applause and honor claim.

They're always on the watch to find
  A plum or goodly prize,
And thrust their fingers deep into
  Their honest neighbors' pies!

JOE, THE CROW-KILLER.

"Joe, Joe, shot a crow,
    And hung it up to dry;
All the boys began to laugh,
    And Joe began to cry."

JOE was not cruel, though he shot
    A depredating crow,
The fate of which was sealed when sped
    The arrow from his bow.

He shot the crow because it stole
    The grain raised by his toil,
And was resolved to put an end
    To any further spoil.

He placed the carcass on a pole
    Conspicuously high,
That other crows might warning take,
    And not the field come nigh.

His playmates young did not discern
    The end he had in view,
While they assembled near the pole
    And round him closely drew.

They laughed at him, and then indulged
    In unrestricted jeers;
Poor Joe did not retort, but sought
    Relief in sobs and tears.

He did not sharply answer them
    And warlike power display,
But bore the taunts without a word,
    Which was the better way.

Thus, when men laugh at us without
    A reason for their sport,
'Tis well the folly should be theirs
    And ours the good report.

THE CAT AND THE FIDDLE.

AN ASTRONOMIC STORY.

——◦◦∙◦◦——

"Hey Diddle-diddle,
  The Cat and the Fiddle,
  The Cow jumped over the Moon;
  The little Dog laughed to see such sport,
  And the Dish ran away with the Spoon!"

"There are more things in heaven and earth, Horatio, than are
dreamt of in your philosophy." — *Shakspeare.*

———

THIS poem brief contains rare gems
  Of astronomic lore,
And tells of wondrous incidents
  We never heard before.

The view of Lyra 't was, perhaps,
  The poet's bosom fired,
And him inclined to note events,
  With melody inspired.

The fiddle's sound, not that of lyre,
   E'er pleasure to us brings,
For of the viscus of the cat
   Is made the music strings!

The stimulating power is in
   The hair of horses found;
For what are strings without the means
   To wake the slumbering sound?

As in the stellar family
   Is found the winged horse,
The Fox and Goose, and Bear and Lion,
   And Bull upon his course,

Why not the timid Cow appear
   Amid the bright array,
Especially when all can see
   There is a "milky way"!

And as a Dipper and a Cup
   Are seen in starlight clear,
It is not strange to common sense
   A Spoon and Dish appear!

No doubt a Dog shines in the sky,
  Clothed with a greenish flame,
Familiar to astronomers,
  And Sirius by name.

It wondrous seems a cow could spring
  And overleap the moon,
And that a dish in sportiveness
  Away should bear a spoon;

But with our optics we can't see,
  With feelings of surprise,
Such things as the astronomer
  Beheld with stronger eyes;

And, too, the joyous canine notes,
  Though to his ear-drum clear,
That came to him through telephone,
  We could not hope to hear!

We must not doubt; events as strange
  Have happened in our time,
And show how sudden is the change
  From comic to sublime.

We know that Venus sometimes has,
  By natural causes borne,
Queen Luna's realm approached, and sat
  Upon her silver horn!

And when the brief sojourn was o'er,
  She slowly moved afar,
And thus passed o'er the pallid moon
  That ever-brilliant star!

Such incidents will e'er delight
  The foolish and the wise,
For Nature is munificent
  With all her vast supplies;

From tender plant to stately tree
  Her beauties are arrayed,
With all the varied forms and fruits
  And floral hues displayed;

From murmuring rill to ocean wild,
  With streams that intervene,
And verdant vales and fertile plains
  And mounts' majestic mien.

The heavens with peace-inspiring power
   Their wonders to us show
In stellar fires and tinted clouds
   And covenantal bow!

And in the sunlit vast expanse
   Between the earth and sky,
Birds, like winged flowers, in joyousness
   Their melody supply.

Though men may doubt, in self-conceit,
   The Nursery story's truth,
It is not so with juveniles,
   With unsuspecting youth.

If they believe such things occurred,
   Rehearsed in language plain,
The annals which such pleasure give
   Were not produced in vain!

·FINIS·